# Stone Cold Heart

## By Stephen Hill

**A Together in the Harvest
Pocket Book**

©1995
by Together in the Harvest Publications
P.O. Box 2050
Lindale, TX 75771

Second Edition
All rights reserved.

Cover illustration and design by Paul Annan

ISBN 0-9637090-1-1

# Stone Cold Heart

## CONTENTS

"A new heart also will I give you, and a new spirit will I put within you: and I will take away the stony heart out of your flesh, and I will give you an heart of flesh."

Ezekiel 36:26

# CHAPTER ONE

## THE DEATH ANGEL COMES

The darkness was deafening.

In my drug-crazed, deathly condition came the voice inside me, "This is it, Steve."

*Am I awake or asleep?* I wondered. *Am I alive or dead? Is this real, or am I hallucinating?*

Slowly, my body began to go into convulsions. *Yes, this must be real! I'm going to die.* I thought. *Just let it happen like everything else in your life. Let death come.*

The thought of dying, of suicide, had daily filled my mind for months. Thinking of getting off the painful treadmill of my life—jail, confusion, hatred, loneliness, hurt and misery— brought the slightest hope and comfort. Drugs no longer offered any high; they could barely fog out the anguish anymore, even momentarily. Hope, love or thinking of others had long gone from me. Yes, death surely would be a relief.

"But it's not happening like I planned," I thought. "It's supposed to be peaceful—a release. Why is this horrible cloud of blackness and pain engulfing me?"

The dawn was breaking, and now my legs and arms were shaking wildly out of control. I couldn't get up and I couldn't relax. Instead of coming peacefully, death was gripping, choking me.

*I can't let this happen. I'm afraid. What will death do to me?*

I could literally feel death's evil—its consuming, devouring power. And now it was saying, "Just give in, just give in, give in."

"No! No!" I cried. Though my body still convulsed in violent agony—one part of me wanted to die, another part wanted to live—my fear was now motivating me to live. Weakly but intently, I began the fight. "No, no, I don't want to die. Mom, Mom, please help me!"

The minutes seemed like hours before my mother came to the room. I could barely tell she was there, for my eyes couldn't focus clearly —and I was still convulsing.

"Son, son!" she cried with fear. "What's wrong with you? You're pouring sweat and shaking!"

Only as her hands touched my hand and forehead did I realize my heart was beating wildly. Momentarily, her touch brought some relief to the violence in my mind.

"Here, I'll get you a cold washcloth for your head," she said. Tears rolled down my face as I waited for her return. What was happening to me?

*I'm hot—no, I'm cold.* Cold flashes sent my body convulsing spastically while my forehead poured sweat. Tears as I had never known them welled up and streamed down my face.

Mother returned, covered me with a blanket and stroked my forehead. I tried desperately to focus to see her.

"What is happening to me, Mama? I'm dying! I'm dying!" I cried again and again. "Help me, Mama, help me! Stop the pain. Somebody, stop the pain!"

But neither of us knew how to stop the pain. Mom tried to make me comfortable, but she could offer only temporary relief. Over and over, she whispered nervously, "Steve, I'm sorry— Steve, I'm sorry. I don't know what to do. I wish I knew what to do!"

"Just stay here—stay with me," I begged. The black cloud of death was grasping me again. It took every ounce of effort to focus my mind on Mom. Every piece of furniture, every picture, every article in the room was covered with death. The walls swelled in and out. It was a nightmare of horror—only I was awake to experience it firsthand.

All day and into the evening it continued, a seeming eternity. Surely, I could not hold out much longer. The clutches of death were toying with me. And all the time, the voice of evil persisted: "Give in, give in. There is no way out. Your life is over, Steve. There is no more. It's time to end it. Let me help you."

It was the voice that over the years I had come to identify as my own. Yet now I recognized it as the voice of deceit—and I cried out: "You're not helping me—you're destroying me. "You're the Destroyer!"

Finally, I had recognized the evil voice as evil. Yet even in this, there was still no relief, no comfort. Mom couldn't help me—and I couldn't bear to have my brother or sisters see me in such a helpless condition.

The pain and agony continued for days. Despite my mom's efforts, I shook and writhed in pain continually. The days were no less painful than the nights. But how endlessly long were those three nights. Mom sat by me hour after hour—but death never left me. The reeking, evil presence surely would soon have me forever.

My thoughts went back to my childhood. If only I had recognized that voice then ...

# CHAPTER TWO

## TWO VOICES AT THE COOKIE JAR

"Steve," Mom called, "Would you like to go outside with your brother and sisters?"

"No, thank you, Mother. It's too cold outside," I answered. The slight chill of the Alabama winter day made me seek the safe, secure refuge of my room and my toys.

With my Lincoln logs, building blocks and erector set to fulfill my creative imagination, I was satisfied and happy. Today I will build a skyscraper, an office, a garage...

Yet my masterful construction was suddenly interrupted. Through the crack under the door came an aroma so sweet, so tantalizing, so powerful, my little body went limp. I dropped the pieces of Lincoln logs.

"What is that smell? Where is it coming from? I've got to find out!"

Rising to my feet, I accidentally kicked over the "Empire State Building"—but that didn't matter. All that mattered to me was finding the source of that aroma.

The sweet aroma totally controlled me. I had become hypnotized by its attraction. And the closer I got to the kitchen, the stronger it got.

Bingo! There in the kitchen, hovering over the stove, was my mom—and directly in front of her on a large tray were twenty-four of the most beautiful, mouth-watering chocolate chip cookies I had ever seen. They were fresh, warm, and—best of all—ready to eat.

My stomach was growling. My mouth was watering. I had to have some of these cookies.

I looked up at my beautiful, loving Mom, and we exchanged smiles. Politely, I said, "Mama, could I have some of these cookies, please?"

Mother continued smiling. She replied, "Son, I'm sorry but you'll have to wait. It's too close to suppertime. You'll ruin your appetite."

I thought, "Ruin my appetite? Who cares? I want some cookies." Forcing a smile, I begged, "Please, Mom, I really want some cookies now. How about just two?'

Mom held her ground. "Not now, Steve. It will ruin your dinner."

In this moment, my whole attitude changed.

11

I was not just hungry—I was mad! That which could satisfy my overwhelming desire was just inches from my nose and mouth. I thought, "Either I get them now while they are fresh, warm and chewy, or I wait until after supper when they're cold and hard. Mama, why are you doing this to me?"

But it wasn't Mama! It was my mind. There was a warfare going on inside. The one voice or power wanted me to do right and the other wanted me to do wrong. It wasn't just with the cookies—it was also there when Mom and Dad wanted me to go to bed, when they told me to take out the garbage, and at other times.

The one power seemed to lean toward obeying my parents, and the other always wanted me to have my own way, no matter what. And now these powers were fighting it out again.

One voice was saying, "Cool it! Obey your mother. Go back to your room. You can have some cookies after dinner."

The other voice argued, "You were in your own room minding your own business when that aroma drew you in here. It's your mother's fault—she made the cookies. The least she could do is give you some."

It was no contest. I gave in to the second voice again. Now it was just to decide how to carry out my will. Should I get mad and holler at Mom? Should I cry and do the "you don't love me" routine? Or, I could grab some cookies and eat them before Mom caught me.

But then that second voice had a better idea: "Wait until Mom is done in the kitchen. When she leaves, sneak back in and take them out of the big, porcelain-pig cookie jar. They'll still be warm and chewy."

Sure enough, in just minutes Mom had gone to her room, leaving the kitchen unguarded. Carefully and quietly, I tiptoed into the kitchen, placed a chair by the counter, climbed up, reached in and grabbed a handful.

Aahh! Success! Back in my room, the stolen treasure was gone within seconds. My stomach was satisfied. But something else was wrong—I didn't feel good inside. I was nervous.

My heart was beating faster than normal. My conscience let me know I had done wrong —I was guilty, I had given in to my selfish voice —but now I didn't like this guilty feeling. I wish it would just go away—but it didn't. Should I just learn to live with it?

# CHAPTER THREE

## THE FOOLISH CHILD

"Stevie, why are you always bothering your sister?" ... "For the last time, Stevie, get in bed and stay there" ... "If you do that one more time, I'm going to have your father punish you...."

What was happening to me? The happy, contented boy with his toys and wonderful parents and brother and sisters was changing. It wasn't intentional. Misbehaving had just become natural.

That same voice—the voice of selfishness and evil that had gotten me the cookies from the cookie jar—had convinced me that he was my friend, the one to lead and guide me. I didn't know that long ago the wisest man on earth had declared with profound understanding that this voice was the voice of foolishness, and only the rod of correction would drive it away.

My parents did try to correct me, constantly. But with four children they did more threatening than spanking, more warning than disciplining. Besides, that voice was helping me become very adept. I only rarely got caught misbehaving. More and more, I appeared to be one kind of child to my parents, another to my brother and sisters, and still another to my friends and classmates.

Who am I? What is life all about? As I moved away increasingly from my parents through my disobedience, life suddenly became complex for me at a tender age. I was faced with more and more decisions about how I should act, who should I befriend and who should I shun, how should I appear, what should fill my thoughts. With so much complexity, it became easier and easier for me to listen and obey the evil voice.

Should I let my mother know that I broke the vase and almost certainly get punished? Or should I lie and say the dog knocked it over and broke it? Soon lying became a habit for me even when lying was unnecessary.

In school, it was easy to glance at a friend's paper to get the answers for the Arithmetic or English test. So why work and study? "Do it the easy way," the evil voice said.

The voice was always there, even at the store after school. There was that fancy, shiny, black cap pistol on the rack. Would Mom buy it for me? She'd probably say, "Stevie, you need to save for it with your allowance." But that would take weeks and I want it now!

I looked around the store aisle. There was no one around. My hands began to sweat, I wanted that pistol so badly. And the evil voice was urging, "Go ahead, take it. They have plenty."

Inside, another voice was also trying to speak. "Stevie, you know that's wrong. That's stealing, and you're going to get into big trouble."

Once again, the evil voice won out. With great paranoia, I eased the cap pistol off the rack and under my shirt. When I slipped out of the store undetected, I told myself, "You did it again. You beat them again. It will be easier next time."

And it was easier the next time—and the next time and the next. Being able to succeed in lies and steal without getting caught seemed to magnify my desire to do more wrong. Shoplifting, burglary, stealing from purses and wallets, cursing, lying and cheating all became part of my basic personality. By the age of twelve, I had put myself in compromising situations and faced fears that many people never experience in a lifetime.

Without exception, my guide had become the evil voice. It boasted, "Just listen to me and you'll never get caught."

Little did I know I was already caught in its web of greed, sin and selfishness. My life was under control—but it wasn't me who was controlling it. Where would this road lead?

By now, I didn't have toy guns, but real ones, along with knives. I had all the candy and the cigarettes, all the clothes I wanted, all the right accessories to impress my friends. So why wasn't I happy? My classmates, even some of the "straights," seemed happy, and yet they didn't have half of what I had. So what was the problem?

I never considered the problem to be who I was listening to and following. My course was taken. It was full speed ahead. Could I ever change my course? Can a leopard change his spots?

# CHAPTER FOUR

## A HEART OF STONE

"Steve," Mom called. "Turn that noise down. It's so loud I can't hear myself think!"

On the radio, my favorite song, "I Can't Get No Satisfaction" by the Rolling Stones, was blasting. It said it all for my generation. Materially, we had everything. But there was still something missing, and we had to get out and search for it, each in our own way.

The decade of the '60s was the age of discovery—of throwing off the old and trying on the new—of searching for new values, new freedoms. As a young teenager, I was much too young to understand or evaluate the politics, ethics, or consequences of it all. But I was old enough to taste and experiment.

What would it feel like to get high—to drink and get drunk? to smoke some marijuana and be stoned? or to flip out on an LSD trip? So many of the older kids were talking about the thrill of doing it. Even some of my classmates bragged that they had tried these new drugs. I didn't know if they were just lying and bragging to "be popular" the way I did, or had really done them.

Yet I knew that soon the opportunity would come and I would give in. "Give in!" the evil voice echoed inside. "It's a whole new world. Everybody is doing drugs. They won't hurt you. You can control them!"

My parents and my teachers had clearly warned me against drug and alcohol abuse. But it was to no avail. Between my rebellious peers and the voice of my "guide," I was hooked before I ever lifted a beer bottle or smoked a joint. Attending the many large rock festivals in our area, seeing thousands of young people such as myself gathered together and getting high made it seem all right.

At home, my brother and sisters acted so good. Why was I the rebel, the black sheep? I thought I was destined to be bad—that I would never "fit in" with my family. I didn't know the truth—that all of us are born in sin and selfishness though we may hide it well from others.

My guilt separated me from receiving any of the love that my family still had for me. I detested being home because it magnified my guilt. So I lived and yearned for going to parties and running with the crowd that was hustling trouble.

At age 13, I was smoking, drinking, smoking marijuana, and even tripping out on pills. These drugs changed my whole way of thinking. I found that the bottle, joint or pill could temporarily eradicate the guilt, eliminate the confusion and deliver me from my feelings of isolation. It didn't matter to me that the feelings induced by these drugs were lies. I didn't care, as long as I could get more to get high again.

The next year I joined a rock music group, the first of many over the next few years. Music was the principal medium of our new lifestyle. We loudly sang songs that spoke of freedom, love, getting high—songs that moved you with feelings of escape. Being in a rock group opened all kinds of new doors for my rebellious lifestyle.

We played at high school dances, pool parties, clubs and private jams where there was always an abundance of drugs and alcohol. I was a young performer, and the attention was fantastic. What a life—continual party! There was always something to do, some place to go, something new to try. It was a season for the pleasures of sin.

Would the party end? Would the ride come to an end? I hoped not. In the uncertain times of the late '60s and early '70s, everyone lived just for the day. By age 16, I had experimented with every kind of drug sold on the street.

School was a fog—total boredom, a waste of time. I no longer kept up with my classmates (except those in the drug culture) because none of that had any appeal. Studies had lost my interest long ago. And enough teachers passed me to get me out of their class that I stayed in school playing the silly games.

Was the ride slowing down? I was now taking more drugs to get high. Our community police were cracking down, and drugs were harder to find and becoming more expensive. More of my friends began quitting school, unable to concentrate on their studies. Many ended up in jail.

Then came the greatest tragedy of my sixteenth year. It happened at the beginning of school one brisk spring morning. I was sitting in home-room period when my name was paged over the school intercom. "Stephen Hill, please report to the principal's office immediately."

What had I done now? Had the police discovered I was selling drugs and were going to arrest me? A hundred thoughts of guilt and fear filled my mind as I made the slow, familiar trek to the school office.

As the secretary showed me into the principal's office, I realized this time was different. The principal had a whole different look today. Something tragic must have happened!

Placing his hands on my shoulders and looking me in the eyes, Mr. Jones said softly, "Steve, your dad has just died. It was a heart attack last night in his sleep. Your mother thought he was just sleeping, but when she tried to wake him, he was gone. I'm so sorry about this. Your neighbor, Mr. Conners, is coming to pick you up."

He just kept looking at me, with his hand still on my shoulder. I guess he assumed that I would cry. But I didn't. I couldn't. I had become so detached, I couldn't think or feel anything. Someone I had known was gone, someone important—but what did it matter?

Being at home in the days after Dad's death was so strange. All those people coming over to console, comfort and share our silence with us.

The voice of conscience pricked my heart for the first time in many months: "You should be helping your Mom in her grief. You're 16, and you should be helping your brother and sisters."

But everything that I thought to say or do was so shallow, so immature. I hadn't realized that besides my emotional detachment from my family, three years of drug abuse had stopped my emotional development—and so I really was shallow and immature.

The solution? It was to get away from these people who were honestly and openly dealing with their hurt and grief. I got up, went to my room, shut the door, and closed myself in from reality.

Soon my friendly, evil voice was back. "Don't worry, Stephen. You really didn't know your Dad all that well. Besides, you're living your own life now. You don't have to cry just because somebody wants you to. In reality, nothing has really changed for you.

"What you need right now are some pills to get you through this time. Don't worry about the feelings for your family. You're different. You can have some help to get you through."

23

The right phone call ... out the back door ... and soon I was hooked up. The painful reality of my dad's death became just a fog. I stayed that way until after the funeral.

I stood there with my flesh-and-blood family while they lowered my father's body into the grave. They were remembering the good times and things, clutching one another closely to fill the void. Yet when our family needed one another most, I couldn't give myself. I was far away. My heart was sealed—cold—a heart of stone. How ironic that the very drug world I had entered to enhance my feelings had now sealed me away so that I couldn't get in touch with even the deepest of feelings.

I had chosen my lot.

# CHAPTER FIVE

## THE DEEPEST DARKNESS

The wisdom of Solomon declares, "The fear of God is a fountain of life to depart from the snares of death."

Through the years Dad had represented at least a semblance of God's authority that bound me to certain rules at home. Now, he was gone and Mom was trying desperately to get her own life back together and care for her children.

It was impossible for my mom to carry out the enforcement of any regulations, though, so I was free to do whatever I wanted. Actually, unwittingly, she was enabling my drug abuse by allowing me to stay in her home with no rules or responsibilities.

Life was a nightmare, full of ups and downs. One day I'd have the desire to excel and make something of myself, but the next day I'd be dragged down, totally wasted, overdosed on drugs. I was constantly being led down the school corridors to the principal's office. Expelled from school—again!

My life was going nowhere. My acquaintances (you couldn't call them friends, because in reality we cared for drugs and highs more than for each other) were sinking lower into death. Many of them had begun using the needle to inject narcotics. Just looking at them, I could see the Destroyer at work. And it should have scared me far away from them. But it didn't. I simply had no other place to go.

Knowing that using the needle would mean physical addiction—and that addiction meant sickness, pain and probably death—I wondered why anyone would do it? Still, it meant getting "higher," "freer"—and I was desperate for some new high, some new meaning, anything. In the end, the voice of self said, "Go ahead. Go along with the others. Just be careful. You can control it. You won't get addicted."

As I melted the morphine into the spoon and drew it into the needle, the last hint of conscience warned, "This will mean destruction to you." But it was too late. The needle pressed against my skin. No one else was making me do it. The evil voice had become me. I said, "Go ahead. Push that needle in." And I did.

As the blood from the puncture dripped

off my arm, my mind made its foggy, hazy way into oblivion. My last thoughts were, "Steve, you are now a full-fledged drug addict. You've become nothing ... nothing ... nothing."

Darkness came, and it became my life—gross darkness and oblivion, my only peace. There was no such thing as controlling my addiction; I lived for the next fix.

To get narcotics demanded more money, which meant more crime, more rip-offs. We became a desperate band of wolves—stealing, devouring. Even our own families weren't safe from our consuming need for money to do drugs. The cycle of drugs-crime-jail, drugs-crime-jail repeated over and over—only to be stopped by death itself.

First, there was Manny. He had come up short once too often in paying our supplier for his heroin. We found Manny one morning with multiple stab wounds in his heart. It was meant to be a lesson to us, but we never were good learners.

Frankie was next. He must have forgotten how much heroin he had put in that last injection. Lying in his girlfriend's arms, he just quit breathing and was gone forever.

Toby self-destructed in a drunken stupor in his car, wrapped around a telephone pole. Similarly, Sammy drove across the wrong side of a highway and met death on the broad side of a truck.

For my good friend, Bobbie, it had all become too much. We were arrested together, but Bobbie never came out on his feet. He hung himself in jail.

Surely, I was on that list, too, somewhere. Where, when, how would it end? I didn't want to think about it. I had to get away—to run, to hide from death. But where?

Without any direction, I began to hitchhike around the country. Wherever I could find shelter became my home—in caves, under bridges, in the desert, and in street missions.

My companions were the refuse of life. Stealing was all we knew, and there was no honor code among us. We'd steal from one another as easily as from a store, home or even a church.

When all else failed, we would end up at the Red Cross office. There was always a line of drug addicts and alcoholics at the clinic to sell blood and get money for a habit. The nurses hid their eyes from ours, as we sold ourselves for the next high.

On that bleak road to oblivion, we met every kind of religious guru and philosopher you can imagine. In our deception and vanity, we argued without end the proper course of life. All the time, we were sitting in the deepest possible pit of muck and darkness. It must have been comical, I'm sure, for people to hear our crazy dissertations and incantations that made no sense to anyone but ourselves.

Solomon had warned that every person has a direction that he feels is right. He honestly believes his illusion. The problem, according to Solomon, is that this illusion will one day end. In the final analysis, many people will find out that their way in life was incorrect, and the result will be eternal death.

Was there a chance I could discover the folly of my life before it was too late?

Would I listen to my mother? No. Would I listen to reality in seeing so many friends die? No. What hope was left? Like a straw floating in the wind, I drifted aimlessly, running from certain death.

One day, a friend and I stumbled onto a

free concert in a large park in Dallas, Texas. Over 5,000 people were there, enjoying the contemporary, positive music. But what appealed to us were the free sandwiches being handed out. Everything was cool until the musicians began to share their message. The guitarist talked about his life before he met Jesus Christ and compared it to his present life as a Christian.

"I was a loser, nobody," he said. "But Jesus came into my heart and changed my whole life. He has given me His all. Every day is wonderful and Jesus has a plan for your life, too. He loves each and every one of you. He wants to forgive you and create in you a clean heart."

To me, this was just another religious guru, trying to convert me to his way of thinking. But to my friend, the guitarist was proclaiming truth. He said, "Steve, I think I'm going up there and talk with that man about Jesus. I want to be a Christian."

I suddenly got angry. "You fool," I shouted at him. "If you believe this garbage about Jesus Christ, and ask for forgiveness, your whole life will be governed by rules and that junk. You won't be able to drink, smoke, do drugs, have sex, curse, or anything else. Besides, all they want is your money."

The venom with which I lashed out surprised me. Why was I so adamant to protect this friend from Christianity? What was it to me if he wanted to change and give up this maddening life?

What was it about this Christianity that upset me? Surely, I had tried just about everything a human being could do in this world. Why was I afraid of this Jesus? Why was I fighting Him?

I pulled my acquaintance in the other direction, and we left the park together. I thought, "That was a close call. No religion is going to control my life with their lies."

"Let's go get high," I suggested. And we did. Darkness reigned supreme again that day.

# CHAPTER SIX

## THE TRUTH STILL SETS MEN FREE

The dry heaving of the drunk in the next bunk was a continual grating on my nerves. The pain and discomfort in my mind and body as I experienced drug dependency made any hope of sleep impossible. But what pressed my mind most at the moment was the dreadful fear of having to fight any or all of the "animals" in this cell-block who might decide to choose me as their next target to rape.

Jail had become my second home. And I quickly had to learn how to survive the inhuman carnage that happens so frequently there. My long, dirty, blond hair and light complexion made me a likely target. So, if I was incarcerated by myself without a friend, I always made a point to befriend some "heavy" by sharing my cigarettes, talking trash, telling about my crimes and planning some new score—even if we were just mostly blowing smoke.

Surviving in the pit of human refuse now became my lifestyle. No longer did I even try to lie and connive my way to get the judge to let me off from punishment for my crimes. This was partly because I usually didn't remember what I had done under the influence of narcotics to end up in jail. Yet somehow, the judges seemed not to want to waste the taxpayer's money on me and usually just gave me a short jail sentence or probation.

When I'd get out, it would be just long enough to commit more crimes for money and get drunk or high before being locked up again. More and more, my thoughts turned to Bobbie, who had hung himself in jail. Maybe that was the only way out. Here I was—I had not yet celebrated my 21st birthday, and my life was over.

My mind and body were burned out. Suicide became more and more appealing. Thoughts of death and the ultimate escape filled my mind. Until...

Until the dramatic Saturday morning of October 25, 1975, when the death angel visited me to take me to my eternal destiny. During those four days, from Saturday to Tuesday, convulsions racked my body while the dark cloud of death hovered over my room, my mind and my life.

Day and night, Mom was there to hold my hand. But only a power greater than both of us enabled me to live through the hellish days and nights. Sometime during this nightmare, two life-changing revelations came to me.

The first was something I'd known as a child, but had long forgotten—that the evil voice that led and ruled me was not me. It possessed and controlled me, but it was not me.

The second, I realized for the first time, was that this evil voice and power was the Destroyer. His intention all along was not to help me, but to destroy me.

Now I no longer wanted that power in me. I wanted to be free from its destruction. But how? Its power held me in bondage. All I could do was lie there and try to resist, knowing that my strength and resistance were failing fast.

On Tuesday morning, October 28, at 10:50 a.m., as I lay in my helpless condition, a knock came on the door. I didn't want to see anyone, but I needed help desperately. Outside my room, I heard my mom open the door to a young man who just a short while before had moved into our city and tried to reach out to me.

He said, "Mrs. Hill, may I please speak with

Steve? I really would like to talk with him."

Mother, who was nearly as desperate as I, replied, "I don't know what's wrong with Steve. He's so sick. I wish we could help him. Maybe you can encourage him in some way."

Mom opened the door to my room and let the young man in. He began, "I know that you didn't want anything to do with me before, Steve. But I've come because you are hurting. I can't help you, but I know somebody who can. His name is Jesus, and He's here with us. He's my best friend, Steve, and He wants to help you."

Tears, that had been bottled up during fifteen years of rebellion, hurt and bitterness suddenly began to flow like a river down my cheeks. The evil presence was still all around me. My body was still racked with convulsions. My mind was still clouded with confusion. But here was someone offering hope.

Still, I was not about to play religious games. He would have to overcome my doubts and unbelief. I protested. "I didn't ever believe in Jesus. I have never prayed to a god in my life. How do I know this Jesus is alive?"

"Steve, you are going to have to trust me in this," he said. "Jesus is here in this room, and

He'll touch your life if you'll just cry out to Him. You don't need to say a fancy prayer. God knows your heart. Just cry out the name, Jesus! Jesus!"

The sound of that name again and again seemed to bring hope from nowhere. The confusion and fear faded slowly as I looked to the ceiling and began to utter that name—"Jesus, Jesus, Jesus, Jesus!!"

And then it happened!!

A peace—a warmth such as I never felt before—filled my body. This power rushed in like a river and took command of everything.

I kept crying out His name, louder and louder: "Jesus! Jesus! Jesus!"

The more I said it, the greater was my deliverance. The convulsions stopped. The evil presence vanished. The pulsating walls in my room stood still!

Almost immediately, I felt the room fill with another presence—this one beautiful and divine. My visitor friend didn't need to tell me what had happened. It was crystal clear—I had just received the gift of new life by Jesus Christ. He had set me free! free! free! free!

For so many years, I had lived in total darkness and bondage to sin. My guilt and sins covered me like a heavy blanket. But nothing is too great for our Lord Jesus Christ. The testimony of God's Word declared, "Though your sins be as scarlet, they shall be as white as snow; though they be red like crimson, they shall be as wool" (Isaiah 1:18). Now, those words were my testimony, too.

The "Destroyer" had held me in his total control. But it was all lies. In truth, there is hope. Life is worth living. I can change—I can be healed. And, as the light of God's love shone into my dark, evil room that morning, all these truths burst in upon my heart in total deliverance. As Jesus said, "You shall know the truth and the truth shall set you free ... For I am the way, the truth and the life. No one comes to the Father but through Me" (John 8:32, 14:6).

Knowing Him wasn't about being religious, going to church, deciding to be good or obeying some set of rules and regulations. It was simply encountering a living relationship with a living God!

On that Tuesday morning, Jesus Christ performed the greatest of all miracles: He transformed my heart. He became more real to me than any other human being. For the first time in my life, I had met the only true God—and He had freed me completely, just as He said: "If you confess your sins, He is faithful and just to forgive your sins and cleanse you from all unrighteousness" (1 John 1:9).

I was clean—forgiven—alive again! The truth had set me free!

# CHAPTER SEVEN

## A NEW VOICE, A NEW GUIDE

There on the parking lot, right in front of my nose, lay a brand-new pack of cigarettes. Not just any pack, but the favorite brand that I had smoked—two to three packs a day—for nearly ten years.

That old familiar voice was saying, "Isn't this luck? Wouldn't one of these taste great right now? It's all right. Nobody is around to see."

There was only one difference between the old Steve and the new Christian Steve, with regard to that voice. Now I had the discernment of the Holy Spirit and recognized that voice as the Destroyer.

Reaching down, I picked up the cigarettes, crumpled them in my fist and said out loud, "Satan, you are not going to defeat me. I am a new creature in Christ. My new nature doesn't need those cigarettes. You are defeated!"

As I began to throw them into a trash can, God's Spirit gently reminded me that they could be retrieved there. I was to leave no room for

Satan to enter.

So I located the nearest public restroom and flushed the pack down the toilet. As I watched them disappear, the Lord spoke to my heart: "Steve, I will always show you a way out of temptation. But you have to be willing to totally destroy every source of temptation, every evil thing that comes your way."

"As you destroy the sources of temptation, your thoughts will be established in me. Remember this truth, and you will be victorious in life."

Sure enough, as I faced head on each of my habits that had controlled my life in the past, such as drugs, alcohol, and cursing, either the relationships were broken because of my stand for Jesus Christ, or people were won to Christ. Within weeks, I was separated from every drug pusher or user friend. It was as if the word "Jesus" spoken in love and respect made them scatter. As is true in football, the best defense of our faith is a good offense—that is, stepping out and witnessing for His name.

The other old habits of lying, hatred and lust all fell away as I changed what I read, what I said, what I did, and who I spent my time with.

The Bible says, "You newborn babes in Christ, desire the sincere milk of God's word, that you may grow thereby" (1 Peter 2:2). That meant me! The Holy Bible became my map in life. To me it was a guide to treasure—more treasures, in fact, than I could possibly imagine. In every page I found the most wonderful promises from God.

I prayed, "Oh, Lord, I've missed so much. I've wasted so many years, and now I'm just like a baby. If You are going to restore me and rebuild me, You'll have to guide me every step of the way, because I don't know what to do."

God did guide me—but not in the way I expected. Within a few short weeks after my conversion, an event took place that radically changed the course of my life. On a cold Saturday night at 11 p.m., a knock came at my door. I answered and found myself face to face with a local narcotics agent. He had in his hand four warrants for my arrest on felony charges. I was handcuffed and led off to jail.

My mom watched as her son once again was being imprisoned. The question entered both of our minds. Why? Why now, God? Steve had changed. He was a new person. These felony charges for drug sales were from his past. Why, God?

The Bible says, "All things work together for good to them that love God and are called according to His purpose." It also says, "His ways are not our ways, His thoughts not our thoughts." God was teaching me how to trust Him.

I spent months in jail, caged like an animal, before I began to see the Lord's purpose. While incarcerated, a minister, Jim Summers, came by to visit on a regular basis. Jim had a drug rehab program called Outreach Ministries of Alabama. Through conversations with the judge and my lawyer, he was trying his best to have me probated into the program. Outreach Ministries was affiliated with Teen Challenge, another drug rehab program, and both were dedicated to helping give spiritual direction and discipline to young men and woman such as myself. If it worked out, I would spend three months with Outreach Ministries and nine months at Mid-America Teen Challenge in Cape Girardeau, Missouri.

My heart pounded and my palms were sweaty as I stood before the judge awaiting my sentence. I deserved years in the penitentiary for these crimes. He had seen me so many times before. Each time I had failed. He had always been lenient, giving me probation. This time I was ready to go to prison.

Calmly raising his eyes from the bench and sternly looking my way, the judge said, "Stephen Hill, this is against my better judgment—but I sentence you to Outreach Ministries. If you do not successfully complete the program, you will spend years in the penitentiary."

I'll never forget that moment. The Lord had made a way out for me!

In Teen Challenge, I learned to put feet to my faith. I learned to live out my professions of love and faith in Christ. I was established in the basics—being water-baptized, being filled with the Holy Spirit, learning how not just to read but to study the Bible and become disciplined in prayer.

It was there I learned that outward actions or words do not dictate where a person is with God. Some guys had all the right religious words and "moves," but they were still playing games with God. Others had genuinely repented of their sins and had come to God, but had not yet learned godly speech and manners. It was the heart condition that God looked at, and only He could give a new heart: "And I shall give them one heart, and shall put a new spirit within them. And I shall take the heart of stone out of their flesh and give them a heart of flesh" (Ezekiel 11:19)(NAS).

God gave me not only a new heart but also a new mind. My mind had become a sewer—filled with garbage, lust, hatred, bitterness, despair, and the like. And when Jesus set me free, forgave my sins and came into my heart, He cleansed me of all the filth in my conscious mind. But there was still a whole sea of subconscious garbage that needed cleansing and renewing.

At first, I let the devil hound me with condemnation every time that old thinking surfaced. Then I learned that I could personally come to Jesus and ask for forgiveness and cleansing—anytime, day or night. In fact, God used those old thoughts for good, because every time they came up, they pointed me to Jesus for forgiveness, and made me love Him even more for His free grace through the Cross. I learned that giving myself, my heart, to Him was not a one-time thing but a continual process: "I urge you therefore, brethren, by the mercies of God, to present your bodies a living and holy sacrifice, acceptable to God, which is your spiritual service of worship. And do not be conformed to this world, but be transformed by the renewing of your mind, that you may prove what the will of God is, that which is good and acceptable and perfect" (Romans 12:1-2)(NAS).

My background had led me to believe that God was a Sunday-morning-church phenomenon. But I learned that He was with me always —that His presence and power were just as available on the streets on Saturday night as in church on Sunday morning.

What thrilled me most at Teen Challenge however, was learning to win souls. I had always looked at Christians as squares and duds. What could be exciting about being good? Then I discovered through the power of the Holy Spirit that we could wage spiritual warfare and be victorious in Christ—that "the kingdom of God (God's rulership) suffers violence and the violent take it by force" (Matthew 11:12).

Through prayer, we saw God do miracles. Men that were crippled were healed. Others diagnosed as manic depressives and subjected to lifetime sedation were supernaturally delivered. But the greatest miracle was to see God soften a street-hardened drug addict's heart before our eyes—to see that person kneel before the Lord in the street and weep tears of joy at finding Christ's forgiveness for the first time. What could possibly be more important, more exciting, than to change the eternal destiny of a life from hell to heaven, to gain an eternal friend, and eternal soul for Jesus? This was the greatest miracle!

For days and weeks, the joy of soul-winning almost burdened me. Why didn't all Christians feel as I did? Why weren't all believers totally dedicated to winning souls? What could possibly be more important? If God could use an ex-burned-out drug addict like me to win souls, surely anyone could be used. Why weren't there more evangelists and missionaries?

Early one morning, I sat on my bed meditating on one of my favorite Scripture passages, Matthew 9:36-37: "When Jesus saw the multitude, He was moved with compassion for them because they were weary and scattered, like sheep having no shepherd." Then he said to His disciples. "The harvest truly is plentiful, but the laborers are few. Therefore pray the Lord of the harvest to send out laborers into His harvest,"

I prayed the prayer that had been stirring for days in my heart: "Lord, could You possibly use me to reach souls for Your kingdom? If You will do this, I will dedicate my life, my all to Your service!"

As I waited and listened for what my God would say, I was almost afraid that perhaps I would be rejected. Instead, God's peace and assurance spoke to my heart: "Son, I am your God and I will work in and through you greater things than you can think or imagine, if you remain humble and obedient."

What would the future hold? I just knew it had to be exciting!

## CONCLUSION

Many years have passed by since that incredible Tuesday morning in October of 1975. Life has become an adventure since then. Every day I discover more of the love of God and His plan for me.

In April 1979 the Lord blessed me with a wife—a woman who had lived a similar lifestyle, had come out victorious in Christ Jesus, and who shares my dreams for the future. Jeri and I met at Bible School, an ideal place to spend time together seeking God for direction. Since graduation, we have taken the love of God to thousands in the United States and on foreign soil.

We have discovered that the same Jesus Christ who changed our lives years ago is alive today—and He radically saves and heals on the streets of New York, Chicago, and Los Angeles. The same Holy Spirit who touched our lives also touches the lives of young and old throughout the United States. The same love of God that penetrated our hearts is available to our poverty-stricken neighbors in the slums of Mexico. The same forgiveness that we've received is available for the millions in Canada, Argentina, England, India, Japan and Africa.

You see, people are the same everywhere you go. Languages change, customs differ, but the heart is the same in every culture. The Bible says that the human heart is "deceitfully wicked!" Only God can change it.

Please allow me a moment more to speak directly to you. Perhaps you picked up this book out of curiosity. You've read it, and now you've been touched by the message. Or maybe a friend gave it to you, hoping you would catch a glimpse of the love of Jesus Christ. However it happened, it wasn't by mistake. The message in this book can change your life.

Are you tired? Are you looking for true happiness and peace of mind? Can you relate to some of the heartache and desperation that I felt in my life?

Here are a few simple steps leading to forgiveness and new life. Read them, act upon them, and allow the love of Jesus Christ to remake you into the person He wants you to be.

## 1. BELIEVE CHRIST IS YOUR FRIEND AND THAT HE CARES ABOUT YOU.

"Casting all your care upon him; for he careth for you" (1 Peter 5:7).

"For we also once were foolish ourselves, disobedient, deceived, enslaved to various lusts and pleasures, spending our life in malice and envy, hateful, hating one another. But when the kindness of God our Savior and His love for mankind appeared, He saved us, not on the basis of deeds which we have done in righteousness, but according to His mercy, by the washing of regeneration and renewing by the Holy Spirit" (Titus 3:3-5) (NAS).

"Henceforth I call you not servants; for the servant knoweth not what his lord doeth; but I have called you friends; for all things that I have heard of my Father I have made known unto you" (John 15;15).

"Jesus...said unto them, They that are whole have no need of the physician, but they that are sick: I came not to call the righteous, but sinners to repentance" (Mark 2:17).

**"For the Son of man is come to save that which was lost"** (Matthew 18:11).

## 2. CALL UPON HIM FOR HELP—NOW!

**"For the scripture saith, Whosoever believeth on him shall not be ashamed. For there is no difference between the Jew and the Greek: For the same Lord over all is rich unto all that call upon him. For whosoever shall call upon the name of the Lord shall be saved"** (Romans 10:11-13).

**"Come unto me, all ye that labor and are heavy laden, and I will give you rest. Take my yoke upon you, and learn of me; for I am meek and lowly in heart: and ye shall find rest unto your souls. For my yoke is easy, and my burden is light"** (Matthew 11:28-30).

## 3. BELIEVE HIM TO SAVE YOU FROM SIN, DEPRESSION, AND FEAR.

**"Verily, verily, I say unto you, He that hearest my word, and believeth on him that sent me, hath everlasting life, and shall not come into condemnation; but is passed from death unto life"** (John 5:24).

"If thou shalt confess with thy mouth the Lord Jesus, and shalt believe in thine heart that God hath raised him from the dead, thou shalt be saved" (Romans 10:9).

"Who (The Father) hath delivered us from the power of darkness, and hath translated us into the kingdom of his dear Son" (Colossians 1:13).

"God hath not given us the spirit of fear; but of power, and of love, and of a sound mind" (2 Timothy 1:7).

## 4. BELIEVE HE WILL CLEANSE YOU AND MAKE YOU OVER AGAIN.

"But if we walk in the light, as he is in the light, we have fellowship one with another, and the blood of Jesus cleanseth us from all sin. If we confess our sins, he is faithful and just to forgive us our sins, and to cleanse us from all unrighteousness" (1 John 1:7,9).

"Therefore if any man be in Christ, he is a new creature: old things are passed away: behold, all things are become new" (2 Corinthians 5:17).

## 5. CONFESS HIM PUBLICLY AS YOUR LORD AND SAVIOR.

"Whosoever therefore shall confess me before men, him will I confess also before my Father which is in heaven. But whosoever shall deny me before men, him will I also deny before my Father which is in heaven" (Matthew 10:32, 33).

"Whosoever shall confess that Jesus is the Son of God, God dwelleth in him, and he is God" (1 John 4:15).

"For with the heart man believeth unto righteousness; and with the mouth confession is made unto salvation" (Romans 10:10).

## 6. TRUST HIM WITH SIMPLE, CHILDLIKE FAITH.

"And Jesus called a little child unto him, and set him in the midst of them, and said, Verily I say unto you, Except ye be converted, and become as little children, ye shall not enter into the kingdom of heaven" (Matthew 18:2,3).

"For by grace are ye saved through faith; and that not of yourselves; it is the gift of

**God"** (Ephesians 2:8).

"But without faith it is impossible to please him: for he that cometh to God must believe that he is, and that he is a rewarder of them that diligently seek him" (Hebrews 11:6).

"That he would grant you, according to the riches of his glory, to be strengthened with might by his Spirit in the inner man; that Christ may dwell in your hearts by faith; that ye, being rooted and grounded in love, may be able to comprehend with all saints what is the breadth, and length, and depth, and height; and to know the love of Christ, which passeth knowledge, that ye might be filled with all the fullness of God. Now unto him that is able to do exceeding abundantly above all that we ask or think, according to the power that worketh in us... unto him be glory..." (Ephesians 3:16-21).

"Therefore being justified by faith, we have peace with God through our Lord Jesus Christ" (Romans 5:1).

**Pray this simple prayer, in faith:**

*Dear Lord Jesus, with my mouth I confess my sins, my emptiness, my selfishness. Forgive me; cleanse my heart and give me a new beginning. I receive You as the Lord of my life. I give You my confidence, here and now. And with Your help, I will let You recreate me into a new person. I believe what the Bible says is true, and I'll act upon it. In Your name I pray, Lord Jesus. Amen.*

Locating a strong Christian church in your community is extremely important. Bible study and fellowship are just two of the many benefits of being a part of a local body of believers.

We'd love to help you more. Please give us a chance.

For more information on the Christian Drug Rehabilitation Program nearest you or if you would like to correspond with Stephen Hill, please write:

STONE COLD HEART
P.O. BOX 2050
LINDALE, TX 75771

**Stone Cold Heart** is also available in the following languages:

Spanish
Russian
Czech
Swedish
Turkish

For more information, please contact us at:

Together in the Harvest
Publications
P.O. Box 2050
Lindale, TX 75771